This *LADYBIRD TALE*
belongs to

....

The
Big Pancake

Retold by Vera Southgate M.A., B.COM
with illustrations by Marina Le Ray

LADYBIRD 🐞 TALES

ONCE UPON A TIME there was a mother who had seven little boys – seven, hungry, little boys.

One day, the mother began to make a very big pancake for her seven, hungry, little boys.

She took flour, salt, eggs and butter and mixed a batter.

Then she melted some butter in her biggest frying pan.

Then the mother poured the
batter into the big frying pan.
It made a very big pancake – a
huge pancake – to feed seven,
hungry, little boys.

The seven little boys watched
the pancake as it cooked.

"We are hungry," they said.
"Is the pancake ready yet?"

Their mother lifted up one
side of the pancake and
looked underneath.

"It is just turning golden,"
she said.

"Is it ready to eat?" asked the seven little boys.

"Oh, no!" said their mother, "I must toss it yet. I must toss it up in the air to turn it over, so that the other side will turn golden. Then it will be ready!"

"Oh dear!" thought the pancake. "I must not wait until my other side is golden or I shall be all eaten up by seven, hungry, little boys. And that will be the end of me! I will run away," thought the pancake. "Yes, I will run right away from seven, hungry, little boys."

The mother took the frying pan in both hands and tossed the pancake high in the air.

Then she held out the frying pan ready to catch the pancake as it turned in the air.

"Oh, no you don't!" said the pancake to itself. It gave a flip in the air, missed the frying pan and landed on the floor.

Then, with one side golden and the other side pale, it rolled away on its edge, like a very big penny.

The pancake rolled out of the door and away down the road.

"Stop!" shouted the mother, her frying pan still in her hand.

"Stop!" she shouted, as she ran after the pancake.

Faster and faster rolled the pancake, away down the road.

The seven, hungry, little boys
ran down the road behind
their mother.

"Stop!" they shouted. "We want
to eat you!"

"Oh, no!" said the pancake as
it rolled on, faster and faster.
"I don't want to be eaten by seven,
hungry, little boys."

Soon the pancake passed a man.

"Stop!" shouted the man.
"You look like a delicious
pancake. Please let me eat you."

"Oh, no!" said the pancake.
"I don't want to be eaten.
A mother couldn't catch me.
Seven little boys couldn't
catch me. And I won't let
you catch me!"

Then the pancake rolled on, faster and faster.

The man joined in behind the seven, hungry, little boys and the mother. And they all ran after the big pancake.

Soon the pancake passed a cat.

"Stop!" shouted the cat.
"You look like a delicious
pancake. Please let me eat you."

"Oh, no!" said the pancake.
"I don't want to be eaten.
A mother couldn't catch me.
Seven little boys couldn't
catch me. A man couldn't
catch me. And I won't let
you catch me!"

Then the pancake rolled on, faster and faster.

The cat joined in behind the man and the seven, hungry, little boys and the mother.

And they all ran after the big pancake.

Soon the pancake passed
a cockerel.

"Stop!" shouted the cockerel.
"You look like a delicious
pancake. Please let me eat you."

"Oh, no!" said the pancake.
"I don't want to be eaten.
A mother couldn't catch me.
Seven little boys couldn't
catch me.
A man couldn't catch me.
A cat couldn't catch me.
And I won't let *you* catch me!"

Then the pancake rolled on,
faster and faster.

The cockerel joined in behind the
cat and the man and the seven,
hungry, little boys and the mother.

And they all ran after the
big pancake.

Soon the pancake passed a duck.
"Stop!" shouted the duck.
"You look like a delicious
pancake. Please let me eat you."

"Oh, no!" said the pancake.
"I don't want to be eaten.
A mother couldn't catch me.
Seven little boys couldn't
catch me.
A man couldn't catch me.
A cat couldn't catch me.
A cockerel couldn't catch me.
And I won't let *you* catch me!"

Then the pancake rolled on, faster and faster.

The duck joined in behind the cockerel and the cat and the man and the seven, hungry, little boys and the mother. And they all ran after the big pancake.

Soon the pancake passed a cow.

"Stop!" shouted the cow.
"You look like a delicious pancake. Please let me eat you."

"Oh, no!" said the pancake.
"I don't want to be eaten.
A mother couldn't catch me.
Seven little boys couldn't
catch me.
A man couldn't catch me.
A cat couldn't catch me.
A cockerel couldn't catch me.
A duck couldn't catch me.
And I won't let *you* catch me!"

Then the pancake rolled on,
faster and faster. The cow joined
in behind the duck and the
cockerel and the cat and the man
and the seven, hungry, little boys
and the mother. And they all ran
after the big pancake.

Soon the pancake passed a pig.

"Where are you going in such a hurry?" asked the pig.

"I am running away from a mother; seven, hungry, little boys; a man; a cat; a cockerel; a duck and a cow," said the big pancake. "They all want to eat me and I don't want to be eaten up."

"Of course you don't want to be eaten up!" said the pig, as he ran along beside the pancake. "I never heard of such a thing!"

Soon the pancake and the pig came to a river.

"Now, what am I going to do?" the pancake asked the pig. "I can't swim!"

"But I can swim," said the pig. "You get on my snout and I'll take you across the river."

So the pancake rolled onto the pig's snout. Then the pig opened his mouth and gobbled up the pancake.

And it *was* a delicious pancake!

That was the end of the big pancake.

So the mother and the seven hungry, little boys and the man and the cat and the cockerel and the duck and the cow never *did* catch the big pancake!

A History of
The Big Pancake

The Big Pancake is a cumulative tale, where the events of the story quickly follow one after another, and build up to reach a dramatic conclusion! With its rhyme and repetition, *The Big Pancake* means it is still a popular tale with children all around the world today.

The Big Pancake was originally included in Peter Christen Asbjørnsen and Jørgen Moe's collection, *Norske Folkeeventyr* in 1842-1844. Ten years later, in 1854, German brothers Carl and Theodor Colshorn published *Vom dicken fetten Pfannekuchen* (*The Big, Fat Pancake*) in their collection of stories, *Märchen und Sagen*.

It is, however, the version of
The Big Pancake published by Joseph
Jacobs in his *English Fairy Tales*
from 1890, that we know today.

This Ladybird edition, first retold by
Vera Southgate in 1972, is a classic
of its time and helped to bring the story
to a new generation of readers.

Collect more fantastic

LADYBIRD 🐞 TALES

Little Red Riding Hood
9781409311126

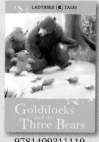

Goldilocks and the Three Bears
9781409311119

Cinderella
9781409311072

Jack and the Beanstalk
9781409311102

The Gingerbread Man
9781409311096

The Three Little Pigs
9781409311089

The Three Billy Goats Gruff
9781409311065

Hansel and Gretel
9781409311133

Puss in Boots
9781409311225

Rapunzel
9781409311195

Rumpelstiltskin
9781409311164

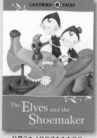

The Elves and the Shoemaker
9781409311188

9781409311171

9781409311218

9781409311201

9781409311157

9780718192556

9780718192532

9780718192549

9780718192587

Endpapers taken from series 606d,
first published in 1964

A catalogue record for this book is available from the British Library

Published by Ladybird Books Ltd
80 Strand London WC2R 0RL
A Penguin Company

001

ISBN: 978-0-71819-254-9

Printed in China